DISCARDED

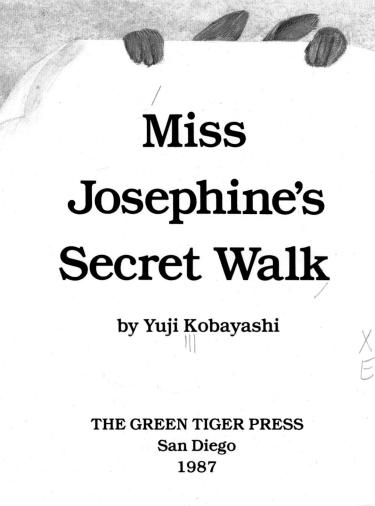

Miss Josephine's Secret Walk

by Yuji Kobayashi

THE GREEN TIGER PRESS
San Diego
1987

"Oh what a beautiful morning!",
says Miss Josephine as she slips
out of bed.

She splashes her face with water, does
her morning business, and trims her
whiskers to make a pretty face.

Puff, puff. She puts on powder.

A touch of lipstick.
A red necklace.
Mother's skirt and hat.

"I feel so elegant.
I must go out."

Agnes sees her, grabs her skirt, and
Miss Josephine tumbles head over
heels.

"Oh Josephine, I'm so sorry," says Agnes.
Little Katy says, "Let's all play together."

They start walking, and as they cross
a bridge they sing,

"Log bridge, log bridge—well, well, well.
Log bridge, log bridge—well, well, well."

WHOOSH!

The water is cold, but it's fun. The three friends float down the river together.

They ride over the waterfall. Miss Josephine's necklace breaks and the beads fly all around.

They shine like drops of dew.

The red beads are now wild berries.
They smell good and taste good:
a little sweet and a little sour.

"It's getting dark!
   Let's hurry home!"

Their mothers and fathers are all
waiting together, and are very worried!
"Where have you been?"
The three friends answer:
"We can't tell! It's our secret!"

The text is set in Bookman by Professional Typography of San Diego, California
Printed and bound in Hong Kong

Original Japanese edition published by
Fukutake Publishing Co., Ltd., Tokyo, Japan 1986
USAGI NO ELNA-CHAN HIMITSU NO SAMPO by Yuji Kobayashi
Copyright © Yuji Kobayashi 1986
English Translation Arranged with Fukutake Publishing Co., Ltd.,
2-3-28 Kudanminami, Chiyoda-ku, Tokyo, Japan

Text and illustrations copyright © 1987 by Yuji Kobayashi
First published by Fukutake Publishing Co., Ltd., Tokyo, Japan
American edition copyright © 1987 by The Green Tiger Press, San Diego, California
First Edition • First Printing
ISBN 0-88138-096-2